A Pocketful of Cricket

A Pocketful of Cricket

REBECCA CAUDILL

Illustrated by Evaline Ness

Troll Associates

Books by Rebecca Caudill

A POCKETFUL OF CRICKET

THE BEST-LOVED DOLL

HIGGINS AND THE GREAT BIG SCARE

SCHOOLROOM IN THE PARLOR

SATURDAY COUSINS

UP AND DOWN THE RIVER

SCHOOLHOUSE IN THE WOODS

HAPPY LITTLE FAMILY

ISBN 0-8050-1200-1 (hardcover)

20 19 18 17 16 15 14 13 12 11

ISBN 0-8050-1275-3 (reissued paperback)

10 9 8 7 6 5 4

For Beulah Campbell,
Boone Companion in the friendly world
of children's books.

This boy, Jay, lived with his father and his mother in an old farmhouse in a hollow. He was six years old.

All around his house Jay could see hills. He could see hills when he stood whittling in the kitchen doorway. He could see hills when he swung on the gate in front of his house. When he climbed into the apple tree beside his house, he could see hills.

Woods covered most of the hills. Corn grew on some of them. On a far green hill, farther than Jay could see, cows ate grass in a pasture.

Every afternoon, in spring and summer and fall, Jay went to the pasture to drive the cows home.

On this afternoon, late in August, he set out before sundown, eating the slice of buttered bread his mother had given him.

He walked along the lane on the side of a hill. The dust under his feet felt soft and warm. He spread his toes and watched the dust squirt between them.

After he had walked forward for a while, he turned around and walked backward for a while. As he walked, he looked at his footprints in the dust.

Queen of the meadow grew on the hillside below the lane. The great pinkish crowns nodded on tall stalks.

A gray spider slept in a web between two of the stalks.

A yellow butterfly sucked nectar from one of the pink flowers. Jay stood and watched it fan its wings—open and shut, open and shut.

A hickory tree grew beside the lane. Its branches cast a dark pool of shade on the hillside. Nuts grew among its leaves.

With a stick Jay knocked a nut from a low branch.

He picked up the nut and smelled the tight green hull that enclosed it. The smell tingled in his nose like the smell of the first frost.

Jay put the nut in his pocket.

A creek flowed across the lane at the bottom of the hill.

Jay waded into the creek.

The clear water rippling against his ankles cooled his feet. It washed them clean of dust.

Jay wiggled his toes in the smooth brown gravel on the bottom of the creek.

He picked up a small flat rock lying in the water. He turned it over. On its underside was the print of a fern.

Jay put the rock in his pocket.

When Jay waded out of the creek he stood for a minute on the bank.

He watched a crayfish scuttling backward among the rocks.

He watched minnows darting about in the water.

At his feet he saw a gray goose feather. He picked it up, smoothed it with his fingers, and put it in his pocket.

A rail fence zigzagged between the creek and a cornfield.

As Jay walked toward the fence he heard a scratchy noise. He saw a gray lizard slithering along the middle rail.

He stopped. He stood very still and watched.

The lizard slithered away, out of sight.

Jay climbed the fence. He sat on the top rail.

He heard the wind rustling in the ripening corn.

He heard bugs and beetles ticking.

He heard a cicada fiddling high notes in the August heat.

He heard an owl hooting in the dusky woods.

On the hill beyond the cornfield he heard a cow bawling.

Jay climbed down from the fence and walked between two rows of corn.

In the dirt he saw an Indian arrowhead, turned up by a plow. He picked it up, brushed the dirt from it, and put it in his pocket.

A woolly brown caterpillar looped fast along a corn blade.

"Why are you hurrying, Caterpillar?" Jay asked.

Beans had been planted with the corn. The vines climbed the tall cornstalks.

Jay picked a bean pod. With his thumb nail he pried it open.

He shelled the beans into his hand. They were white, striped with red speckles. The stripes on every bean were different from the stripes on every other bean.

In Jay's hand the beans felt cool—like morning.

Jay put the beans in his pocket.

At the far end of the cornfield Jay climbed over the rail fence into the pasture.

The cows looked up from their grazing.

Jay walked past the cows. He climbed up the steep pasture hill. The cows went back to their grazing.

An old apple tree stood at the top of the hill. The russet apples that grew on one side of the tree were sweet. The red apples that grew on the other side of the tree were sour.

Jay picked a russet apple with one hand, and a red apple with the other. He took a bite from one apple, then a bite from the other—sweet and sour, sweet and sour.

As he ate, he looked off into the hollow below him. It was long and narrow. A road ran the length of it. At the end of the road stood a white schoolhouse.

Jay looked a long time at the schoolhouse. Then he turned and walked slowly down the hill toward the cows.

The cows looked up once more from their grazing. They switched their tails and started home. Nodding their heads and switching their tails, they walked, one behind another, along the cow path beside the fence.

Jay walked behind them.

Beside the cow path a cricket jumped.

Jay watched the cricket crawl underneath a stone.

Quietly he lifted an edge of the stone.

Quickly he cupped his hand over the cricket.

He gathered the cricket in both hands. Carrying it gently, he hurried after the cows.

Across the creek he waded.

Along the lane he trudged in the dust.

Into the barn he drove the cows. His father was waiting to milk them.

"What took you so long?" asked Jay's father.

"Nothing," said Jay.

Jay hurried to the house.

"What's that in your hands?" asked Jay's mother.

"Cricket," said Jay.

"What are you going to do with him?" asked Jay's mother.

"Keep him," said Jay.

"What will you do with him when you go to school?" asked Jay's mother.

"How many days till I go to school?" asked Jay.

"Five," said Jay's mother. "Next Monday you'll begin."

"Cricket will stay in my room and wait for me," said Jay.

"You'll need a cage to keep him in," said Jay's mother.

She opened a kitchen drawer and took from it a tea strainer. She tucked the handle of the strainer into Jay's pocket.

Off Jay hurried to his room.

He laid the strainer upside down on his table and put Cricket inside.

He brought Cricket water in a bottle cap.

He brought Cricket a piece of lettuce leaf, a thin slice of cucumber, and a slice of banana the size of a nickel.

Cricket sat inside the tea strainer. Jay sat on his bed beside the table and watched.

Cricket sat and Jay sat.

Cricket did not drink the water.

He did not eat the lettuce, nor the cucumber, nor the banana.

"Jay, come to supper!" called Jay's mother.

Jay, on his bed beside the table, watched Cricket.

"Jay!"

After supper Jay hurried back to Cricket.

Some of the lettuce leaf was gone, Jay thought.

A nibble had been nibbled off the cucumber, he thought.

He sat on his bed beside the table and looked at Cricket.

"Do you like your new home, Cricket?" he asked.

Cricket sat and Jay sat.

The light in the room grew dim.

Night came.

Jay pulled the table closer to his bed. He got into bed and fell asleep.

A noise waked him. "Chee! Chee!"

Cricket was fiddling. Cricket was fiddling loud and clear. "Chee! Chee! Chee!"

Jay sat up in bed and listened.

"You do like your new home, don't you, Cricket?" he asked.

"Chee! Chee! Chee!" fiddled Cricket.

Jay reached under his pillow and found his flash-light.

He turned the flashlight on. The fiddling stopped.

Jay turned the flashlight off and put it under his pillow.

He lay down again. In the dark he waited, listening . . . listening.

"Chee! Chee! Chee!" fiddled Cricket.

The next day Jay made Cricket a cage out of a piece of wire screen. It was bigger than the tea strainer.

Every morning Jay brought Cricket fresh pieces of lettuce and cucumber and banana. He put fresh water in the bottle cap.

Every afternoon Jay shut the door of his room, turned Cricket out of his cage, and played with him.

Cricket jumped about the room. Jay jumped after him.

Cricket crawled up the curtain at Jay's window. He jumped to the door of Jay's closet.

"Don't let Cricket in that closet," warned Jay's mother. "He might eat your new sweater. Then what would you wear to school?"

Every night, when Jay got into bed and the dark room grew still, Cricket fiddled.

"Chee! Chee! Chee!" And "Chee! Chee! Chee!"

Monday came.

Jay was ready for school early.

He said good-bye to Cricket. He looked at Cricket a long time.

"You'd better be going now," said Jay's mother. "You mustn't be late for the bus your very first day of school."

Jay said good-bye to his mother. He said good-bye again to Cricket. He started down the road.

When he had gone a few steps he turned and hurried back. He went into his room. He stood looking at Cricket.

"Jay!" called his mother.

Quickly Jay emptied his pocket. He piled on the table an Indian arrowhead, hickory nuts, buckeyes, and beans.

"Jay!"

Into his pocket Jay tucked Cricket. Away he ran down the road.

At the mailbox Jay waited.

Along came the yellow school bus. It stopped, and the driver opened the door. Jay climbed in. He sat down beside a window in the front of the bus.

The bus was filled with boys and girls. A few of them, like Jay, were going to school for the first time. Most of them were big boys and girls. They talked and laughed.

"Chee! Chee!"

Inside Jay's dark pocket Cricket began fiddling.

The talking stopped. Everybody listened.

"Chee! Chee! Chee!" fiddled Cricket.

Jay cupped his hand against his pocket to quiet Cricket.

"Maybe somebody's taking a cricket to Teacher," said a big boy.

Everybody on the bus laughed—everybody but Jay. He cupped his hand harder against his pocket.

"Chee! Chee! Chee!" fiddled Cricket.

"Maybe Towhead down there in front has that cricket," said a big boy in the back of the bus.

Everybody on the bus looked at Jay.

Jay crowded against the window. He pressed his hand hard against his pocket. He looked straight ahead.

"Chee! Chee! Chee!" fiddled Cricket.

"I'd like to see Teacher when that cricket starts singing in school," said a big boy.

Everybody on the bus laughed very loud—everybody but Jay.

When the bus reached the schoolhouse it stopped.

Jay waited until all the other boys and girls had got off. Then, pressing his hand against his pocket, he too climbed off.

He stood wondering where to go.

The driver smiled at him. "You belong in that room just inside the front door," he said to Jay. "Good luck with your cricket!" he added.

Jay looked at the big boys and girls in the school-yard. They were calling to one another. They were laughing and talking.

Jay kept close to the fence as he made his way around them.

He found his room.

He found Teacher inside the room.

He told her his name.

He sat at the desk she pointed out to him.

All around him sat other boys and girls. They were all his size.

Jay kept his hand pressed over his pocket. He sat still and waited.

A bell rang.

Teacher began talking to the children. The children listened. The room was very quiet.

"Chee!" fiddled Cricket.

Jay pressed his hand against his pocket to quiet Cricket.

"Chee! Chee! Chee!" fiddled Cricket.

The children turned in their seats. They giggled.

Teacher stopped talking. She looked about the
room.

"Does someone have a cricket in this room?" she
asked.

No one answered.

Teacher began talking again.

"Chee! Chee!" fiddled Cricket.

Teacher left the front of the room. She walked
up and down between the rows of desks. As she walked,
she talked to the children. As she talked, she listened.

She reached Jay's desk.

"Chee! Chee!" fiddled Cricket.

"Jay," Teacher asked, "do you have that cricket?"

Jay swallowed hard. He nodded his head.

"You'd better put it outside," said Teacher. "It's disturbing the class."

Jay sat very still. He looked at his desk. He pressed his hand hard against his pocket. He felt Cricket squirming.

"Jay," said Teacher, "put the cricket outside."

Still Jay sat. Still he looked at his desk.

"Jay," said Teacher, "aren't you going to put the cricket outside?"

Jay shook his head.

"Why not?" asked Teacher.

"I couldn't find him again," said Jay.

"Put him outside anyway," said Teacher. She waited.

Jay swallowed hard. He glanced up at Teacher. Then he looked at his desk again.

"You could find another cricket, couldn't you?"
asked Teacher.

Jay shook his head. "It wouldn't be this one," he
said.

"Chee! Chee!" fiddled Cricket.

Jay looked up at Teacher.

"Jay," said Teacher, "is this cricket your friend?"

Jay nodded his head.

"I see," said Teacher.

Teacher walked slowly to the front of the room.

"Boys and girls," she said, "every day in the first grade we have what we call 'Show and Tell.' Anyone who has something special may bring it to school to show the class and tell about it. This morning Jay has brought a cricket to class. It is something special. It is his friend. Jay, will you come to the front of the room and show the boys and girls your cricket? You can put him under this glass," she said.

She turned a water glass upside down on her desk.

Jay walked to the front of the room.

He took Cricket from his pocket.

He put Cricket under the upside-down glass.

"Tell the class about your cricket, Jay," said Teacher. "How did you catch him?"

Jay told the class how he had caught Cricket in the cow pasture.

The boys and girls asked Jay many questions.

"How long have you had Cricket?"

"What does he eat?"

"Where does he sleep?"

"How high can he jump?"

"Can he do tricks?"

Jay answered all their questions.

"What makes him sing?" asked a girl.

"He doesn't sing," said Jay. "He fiddles with his wings."

"Tell him to fiddle now," said all the boys and girls.

"He likes to fiddle in the dark," explained Jay. "That's why he was fiddling in my pocket. It's dark in there."

"Does Cricket fiddle especially for you some-times?" asked Teacher.

"Every night," said Jay.

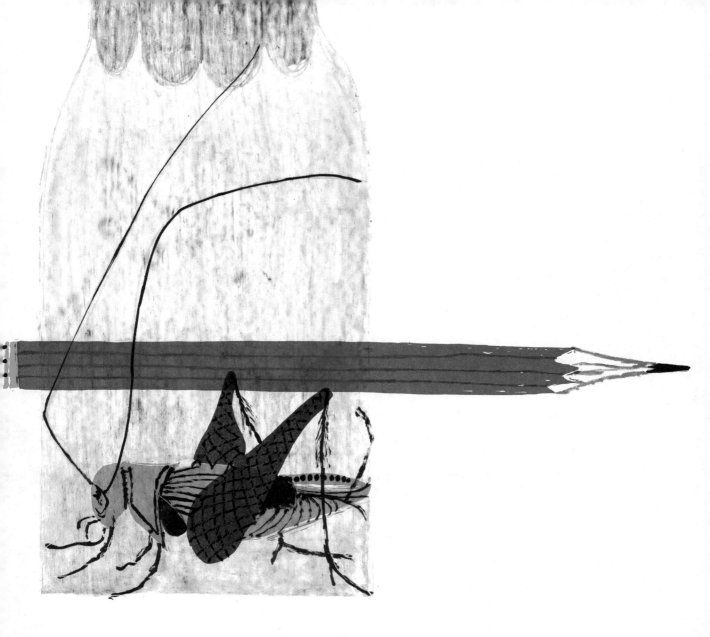

"You may put Cricket back in your pocket now, Jay," said Teacher. "If he fiddles, he won't disturb us. When you have something else special, bring it for 'Show and Tell.'"

"What are you going to bring next, Jay?" asked a boy.

Jay thought of the stone with the print of a fern on one side. He thought of the gray goose feather. He thought of the Indian arrowhead.

He thought of the hickory nut, and of the smell of it that tingled in his nose like the smell of the first frost.

He thought of the beans.

He thought of the cicada fiddling high notes in the August heat.

He thought of the russet apples and the red apples growing on the same tree—sweet and sour, sweet and sour.

He thought again of the beans—white, striped with red speckles, and, in his hand, cool, like morning.

"Beans," he said.